We Hate Rain!

JAMES STEVENSON

GREENWILLOW BOOKS, NEW YORK

E
St

*Watercolors and a black
pen were used for the full-color art.
The text type is ITC Clearface.*

*Printed in Hong Kong
by South China Printing Co.
First Edition
10 9 8 7 6 5 4 3 2 1*

*Library of Congress
Cataloging-in-Publication Data*

*Stevenson, James (date)
We hate rain!
Summary: Grandpa tells Mary Ann
and Louie how he and his brother,
Wainey, coped with a massive
rainfall when they were young.
[1. Rain and rainfall—Fiction.
2. Grandfathers—Fiction] I. Title.
PZ7.S84748Wf 1988   [E]   87-21204
ISBN 0-688-07786-2
ISBN 0-688-07787-0 (lib. bdg.)*

/ / / 7 /

"A rain is what came down that time when my
little brother Wainey and I were young," said Grandpa.

"The first three weeks weren't too bad."
"Three weeks?" said Mary Ann.
"Three or four," said Grandpa.

"Did it stop raining soon?" said Louie.

"Stop?" said Grandpa. "It was just getting started!"

"It was?" said Mary Ann.

"The next week the water was up to the porch.
Our mother and father told us to stay indoors.

Each day the water rose higher."

"In the morning we got up and brushed our teeth

and got dressed.

I practiced the piano

and Wainey rode his tricycle.

We blew soap bubbles

and had diving contests.

We sent things to each other by boat.

"We had difficulty feeding the fish...."

"There were always friends passing through. They floated in one window and out the other.

It was nice, at first.

But then we began to get strangers...

...so Father shut the windows.

We moved up to the second floor,
but the water kept seeping in.

Wainey paddled around in a wooden salad bowl.

When the water reached the attic, we moved up to the roof."

"But finally the box was empty."

"Each of us dreamed our own dreams...."

In the morning we had a big surprise.
The rain had stopped, and the water was gone!"

"Our house was still full of water all the way to the top!

I took a big breath, and dived down the stairs.

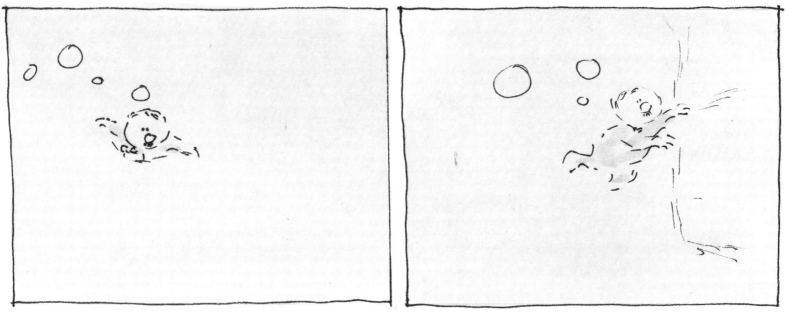

I swam through the house, trying to open the windows. No luck.

I couldn't budge the doors, either."

DID YOU GIVE UP, GRANDPA?

ALMOST. BUT SUDDENLY I HAD AN IDEA...

"I swam into the bathroom   and pulled the plug out of the bathtub.

There was a tremendous noise, and a giant whirlpool

and the whole house was almost entirely dry."